The Kiss & The Bite

47 poems and one short tale

CLIFF BRITTEN

AuthorHouse™ UK Ltd.
500 Avebury Boulevard
Central Milton Keynes, MK9 2BE
www.authorhouse.co.uk
Phone: 08001974150

© 2010 Cliff Britten. All rights reserved.

No part of this book may be reproduced, stored in a retrieval system, or transmitted by any means without the written permission of the author.

First published by AuthorHouse 12/17/2010

ISBN: 978-1-4520-1750-1 (sc)

This book is printed on acid-free paper.

This book is dedicated to all my friends
who read this stuff and gave me the confidence to write.

They know who they are

Contents

DARK

Moods 2
Promises 3
Lonesome tonight 4
Lake 5
Cab Roach 6
Death 7
Fragility 8
Fire 9
Film noir 10
Goodbye 12
Heart Matters 13
My Valentine 14
Mother's Day 15
Patterns 16
Relationships 17
Secret 18
The pain I've felt 19
Vamp It Up 21
The smile 22
What you are 24
A very short poem 25
photo 26
The four 27
Love 29
What's it like? 30
Dream 31
16 lines 32
Zoo 33
The plea 34

LIGHT

Cliff (does it suit) 36
Day out 37
Just desserts 38
Ms Spelt 39
Protective clothing 41
Sweet Fun 42
The Shape of it all 43
Journey 44
Seven Hours 46
Sixteen people 47
Out of this world 48
Fat Bloke 49
Cash crisis 50
Drivel 51
The waiting game 52
World cup .... A repetitive tale 54
New York 55

SHORT STORY - ONE WAY MISSION 57

Dark

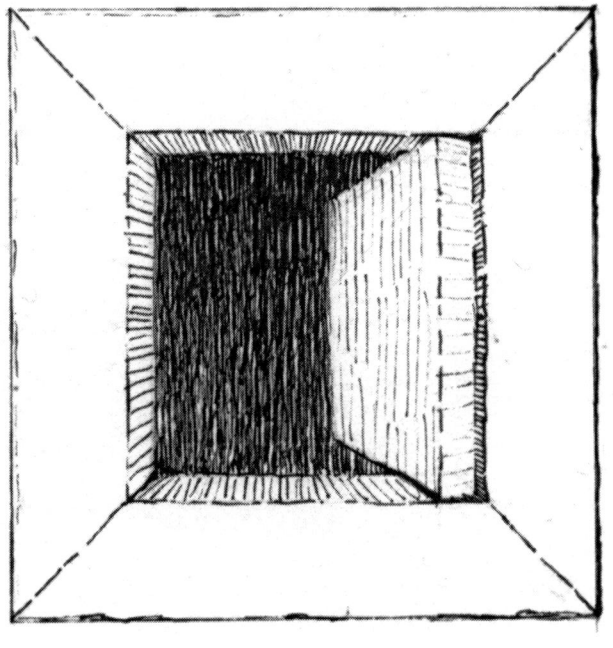

Moods

To talk of moods
Defining our mental state
Black is the worst mood
Dark and brooding
So a good mood must by rule
Be a shade of white
The better the mood
The brighter that white
Mood swings like a pendulum
Vacillating
And then stops, deciding
The mood I feel today?
The colour of a grey felt tip
The one in a pack of eight
Good or bad?
Moderate, I think
Another day meets
The other shades
Flowing either way
To their black or white Parameters
Nameless, intangibles
Unbroken tones
Waiting patiently
To be chosen

For the next dance

Promises

Promise me a gift, she said

The gift is my promise, he said

My promise costs nothing

Whatever I promise

A temporary state

A lie in waiting

Do you still want it?

It may be worthless

Take your pick

The promise… to do

The promise….I will

The promise…to be

The promise to stay

The promise a prop for your failings

Uttered words in a sentence

Held in pointless reverence

Will you?, Can you?, please promise

I promise, I promise, I promise, he said….

To break my promise

Lonesome tonight

Love is a many splendoured thing

Who wrote that?

Certainly not me

If I did, It would read

Love is a pile of shit

That you don't need

It'll make you bleed.

That "splendour"

Where did he get that from?

Was it a "him"?

Sounds a bit "her" though

I just can't remember

Splendour doesn't work… so

Was he or she on the opium?

Living in cotton wool Librium

Pink satin sheets and

Heart shaped cushions

Furry bears and button eyed kittens

Try living in my wire wool land

That's rough on the skin

The place with no SPLENDOUR

The place without

The opposite gender

Lake

I feel like you today, flat and blue

But I am depressed

So that's why

And you are a lake in summer

Beautiful and serene

Yet we are the same you and I

We like our solitude

If disturbed

We freak, sending our feelings outward

Spiralling to far off boundaries

Shaking, trembling

No longer tranquil

But an ordered mess

Everyone leave us alone

In our isolation

Let us be still once more

Still, flat and blue

In the hot summer

Cab Roach

At dark of night they come to hunt in hordes
 Shiny black shells reflect synthetic light
Strong and bold and very self-assured
In masses please observe their might

The streets belong alone to them
Scavenging all that lay in wake
Gathering to dance a requiem
One thought alone to take, take, take

Orange eyes flicker their approach
Metallic heavy pincers open wide
Disgusting, vile march of the roach
Burnished, polished, lustrous they glide

Victims claimed inside this hideous shell
Stripped and bared of all that they possess
The roach emits a heavy leathery smell
Captor in a state of acquiesce

Regurgitate the victim when fulfilled
Of all except the wherewithal to live
No remorse or passion do they yield
Selfish with no regard to give

They thrive while ravaging our kind
Increase their numbers, stronger they become
Moral compass always ever blind
And always we the scapegoat must succumb

Death

I find it hard to attract

Attracting you is easy

I resist your advances

And yet you wait

Patience you show

You know I think of you

My musing's not lustful.

But fear inherent

Selfish, selfish whore

You will end my joy

Break my feeble heart

And take your one embrace.

Fragility

Don't touch me too hard,

I have a hairline crack

Translucent skin, like paper

Erratic heartbeat laid bare

If you touch me I will break

And shatter into a thousand bits

Each piece part once of the complex me

No longer composite, now just raw

I'm made of tears, always primed

Waiting for the order, to go over the top

Expose myself to the enemy

Don't touch me too hard,

I swear I will break.

Fire

I am the warmth to children at camp
To those cold in the night.
 I bring relief
Light and heat my maxim

Know my rules of physic and math
For I can and will change
Destroy you all
Half a continent

I am God in fact, in a brazen coat
All consuming
Strutting my flamboyant dance
Across the earth

I will inhale
A giants breath
See my colours of every hue
My shapes, my power

I like to show off in a painted coat
I wear it well, It is a playful act for now.
But believe this
Do not play with matches
Or me.

Clifford Britten

Film noir

Hitchcock or Wilder, where to start
Long shadows glimpsed in black and white
The film noir such perfect art
The mood, the dialogue ever tight

Tilted hats and femme fatale
Ménage a trois deceit and greed
Someone's gonna end in jail
Film noir plants the perfect seed

The image planted in our head
Narrative overlay, perfect tone
That cool blonde will soon be dead
Double indemnity stands alone

Strangers meeting on a train
The meet, the deal, the double-cross
To hatch, to scheme and kill in vain
To end in tears at someone's cost

The pounding rain, the atmosphere
Secrets whispered on a phone
The sex, the fifties, the twists the fear
All shot in perfect monochrome

Goodbye

Cold room, cold room
Don't invite me
Your contents
Fill me with dread
I am compelled, I see
Your face framed in oak
Frozen, changed, not you
Look again
I feel ……………………

Warm room, warm room
I see
Your face, my mother
Let me stay
Forever…………………..

Heart Matters

It's hard to keep a rhythm
When every line is trite
But the banality of the words here
Seems to parody our life

I will never use a cliché
 When my heart is on my sleeve
Two hearts used to beat as one
I can hardly breathe

They say you hurt as much as me
 But the ball is in your court
You hold all the aces
 In matters of the heart

My Valentine

You'll be my Valentine

Of a darker red
My selfish Valentine

I'll shower you with fake affection
Empty gifts I will bestow
Your love will grow
A tangled twisted thing
To suffocate my soul

You'll be my Valentine
Of a chronic love
My vile Valentine

Your counterfeit letters I'll dissect
On evil Satan Day

Mother's Day

You didn't want to leave

No choice for you

I said I would visit

With penned words

Cemented with tears

On purple paper

We never spoke again

You unable to return

My visits rare and short

Not in that script

Even today, your day

The day I promised

Promised, promised

Shame is my charge

Accept these few prose

To know I don't mean it

Such is the nature

Of death and the grave

Patterns

I need a drink
No not need, just want a drink
A nice long, cold drink, just one
To help me think

I need some coke
Not need, just want some coke
A lovely, lazy long fat line of coke
Feel it moving to the back of my throat

I need a whore
No not need, yes need a whore
A naughty, rude, sexy whore
Uninhibited session of rampant sex
And then to leave her wanting more

I need some meth
Yes need, need, need some crystal meth
Those shards of glass of perfect meth
To rise and trip and float an' all
I know Im gonna feel like death

I need to sleep
Yes must have sleep, must I said
A long unbroken dreamless sleep
The curtain of that blackened home
Please help me I've got in too deep

I must get up,
I gotta think
Don't want or need to, but must just think
The barren day that lies in wait
How long I've been in shredded wheat
God help me I just need a drink

Relationships

Search
Find
Fancy
Talk
Meet
Laugh
Joke
Talk more
Promise
Have sex
Have sex again
Have more sex
Talk less
Argue
Have sex
Promise less
Have less sex
Argue more
Shout
Scream
Don't laugh
Cry
Don't have sex
Finish
Repeat ad nauseam

Secret

I seemed to have died yesterday

In the early evening

So emotional

It's okay though, I like it

I did it on purpose

You have to concentrate, focus

It's very demanding indeed

This being dead game

It gets easier though

Once you know the secret

Oh yes

The secret is,……….

Realising how awful it is

To be alive

The pain I've felt

The pain I've felt in life is as follows

3 car crashes, 2 broken noses

Nose job to rectify, cracked sternum

Bit off tip of tongue, smashed teeth into lips

Fractured wrist, many burns

Torn ligaments, numerous cuts

Many bruises, fingertip sliced

Attacked with snooker cue

Caught finger in jigsaw (motor on)

Metal rod poked in eye (accident)

Multiple stitches, cycle crash

Motorbike crash, scraped skin off back

Stones embedded in knee

Few scars… Clearly

The pain caused is all down to friction

One force against another

How ironic then,

The most pain I've ever felt,

When your hand left mine

Clifford Britten

Vamp It Up

I see the pale, the teeth, the brow
The hollowed cheeks, the tormented frown

You can't see me in the void of glass
I'm looking back through long history past

The mirror knows what's gone before
Fragmented scenes I long abhor

White sheets with red ribbons
Reflect in my eye

Quite dead their deportment
But never to die

Horror, Oh Horror is all that I see
The frozen face in the mirror is me
This is all I'm meant to be

I thirst, but quench will wait awhile
And when sated bring a wretched smile.

The smile

Fuck this, this is hard

I am trying to fill up hours

Some sort of vigil

I am very unhappy

Drunken stupor please

No, a better person now

Do I need penance?

Have I wronged someone?

Not as far as I know

Why this then

Must be a reason

Oh I get it

Its part of the pattern

No one can stay happy

It is a crazy state

Temporary

I've had my time

And now the antithesis

All time is stretched now

My life compressed

So much time

Nothing to do

That is not my style

I must find a mirror

Check myself out

See if I have a crooked mouth

Maybe a tear or two

Consider my torpor

The face so blue

Bring it back, please

That inane grin

The sarcastic smirk will do

Anything resembling

A Smile

What you are

Collection of cells, much bone

Blood, some guts, sinew, skin

Hair, grey matter, fluids inc.

Snot, sweat etc

This view makes it easy for me

To put you in perspective

But in reality and truth

You are

A carefully constructed thing

Just enough of all of the above

In all the right ratio

For any one to love

Snot, sweat included

The grey matter was the thing for me.

Oh, and the red hair!

A very short poem

I am, I am, I am, I said

That's what you say when you're not dead !

PHOTO

Caught and surrounded by 4 chrome lines

In that brief instant of your life

Not contriving, nor posing but so unaware

Of the power of your nonchalant stare

Where, why, what were your thoughts

In that far away gaze?

What had happened before you were iced in that frame?

And just after that moment were you ever the same?

I see you quite clearly, your beauty and poise

Searching for answers, to just hear your voice

Someone had stolen your face on that day

And here I am pausing, rewind and replay

The four

Anguish and misery

A grim duo they pose

Those two chose

To stalk my brain

Outward traits they fail to rein.

Despair and pain

Walk with them

Treading my faith to dust

And me to agonise… those

Masters of disguise

And watch them synchronise

Behind my plastic mask

Await the big reveal

No strength for this ordeal

Love

Do you love me?

But I love you though

How comes you don't?

Still love me…. I mean

Oh! You do love me

But not in that way

How comes, you don't

Love me?

In that way…. I mean

But you do in a way

What way's that then?

I love you in both ways

I hate love

Clifford Britten

What's it like?

When I'm with you

You are like a warm jumper on a damp day

When I feel you its

Like touching a fabric unknown

Your framework, construction

All good

When I see you, it's always like the first time

When we talk its chat show style, fun

Interesting, effortless

When I hold you, it's like holding a baby

With one hand over a bridge

Water rushing beneath

Overwhelming frightening

So when you leave me

What's that like?

Dream

My dreams are frightening
Seriously
Every night
Real horror and gore
Just like in the movies
I, the victim
Chased by grotesque
 Violent Men,
 I can touch them,
Smell their breath
 I run in quicksand
Avoid their grasping hands
The coppery taste of fear
In my throat
They gain ground
Just within reach
I tire, my legs ache
Exhausted, they are upon me
What now, Oh my god
Too awful, I will die
A violent sickening death
Then!!!!!!
In a cold damp sweat
I'm awake
Wide eyes staring
The brown bedroom wall
It was just a dream
Only a dream
And then
The real nightmare begins

Clifford Britten

16 LINES

The line of shirts I chose from

The lines of queues at the station

The line I used (district) Hammersmith

The lines I spoke to charm you

The lines of coke we took

The lines of beer at the table

The line of the banister on the stairs

The line and feel of the handle

The lines of coke we took

The line we chose to go down

The line of your perfect breast

The line of your supple groin

The line and cool cut of your knickers

The lines of coke we took

The line you drew

When you said stop

Zoo

Since you left

I live in a zoo

The polar bear on artificial ice

The monkey without the laugh

The lion with the weakened roar

The zebra on a confined plain

The tiger bereft of prey

The elephant that can't remember

I want to be the urban fox once more

To live in the enchanted toilet

Play by the melted river

Dance with the liquid pixies

Sharing their shrooms

Near the sharpened stairs

In the tightened hallway

By the purple carpets

In the lighted dark

With you x

Clifford Britten

The plea

I m dead to you now

A decaying corpse

Deal with the smell

When the maggots clean up

Clean bone revealed

You can relax, wait for the bell

To ring in your head to tell

You that all memories fade

Eventually

Now I am gone, you are free

Trouble is I'm still here

Agonised,

Can you be dead to me?

Though I love you,

I need closure… the pain

Of you living on

Your mind intact, to feel, to want

It's all too much, I need you gone

I used to say I would die for you

Not brazen bargaining

A brash thing or a plea

In loving you lies the paradox

Can you be dead for me?

Light

Cliff (does it suit)

Cliffs are tall

I am not

Cliffs are straight

I'm not that either

Cliffs are rugged

I'm more smooth

Cliffs hang around near Oceans

I'm a lousy swimmer

Cliffs have a face

As do I

Cliffs are edgy and dangerous

That's more like me

I saw a sign once

It said beware unstable Cliff

I tend to agree

Day out

Stripy deck chairs 50s style

Sandy beach stretch on a mile

Beach huts stand like soldier men

Charley Dickens with his pen

Donkeys trudge their weary way

No respite on a Sunday

Shops containing bric a brac

Loads of stuff stuck in a rack

Machine gun wielding dinosaur

Noddy smiling in his car

Two old ladies "chit a chat"

Broadstairs is a lot like that

Clifford Britten

Just desserts

When I was young and green
I stood proud and firm

A member of the bunch
But now I am old before my time

With yellow skin and stooped demeanour
Brown liver spots cover my all

The rest of the bunch have deserted me now
One at a time to their fate

Soon I too will be stripped naked
My flesh exposed

And then who knows what fate awaits

Sent away on a boat perhaps
Or split in two on a plate

Ms Spelt

I love you, I really do
You have helped me out
I didn't know you would
But you have come through
Time and time again.
So selfless.
I turn you on
My fingertips caress
Your sleek black body
So responsive to my touch
You are my crutch
My keyboard, my release
You are a poet, an artist
The tap, tap, tap
Instead of the
Smack, smack, smack
Of my head against the wall
You have soothed me
You have moved me
To distraction, interaction
Here we are again you and I
In unison, my thoughts
Your neat mutation to the page
It's all you, really it is
I just couldn't cope,
Without you by my side

Clifford Britten

Protective clothing

You can wear my shiny suit

It sparkles in the night

It's made of special stuff

And it's got love inside

Clifford Britten

Sweet Fun

Watching her eat took me back,

Great handfuls from the bag

Cheeks full and round,

No more room in there,

Head back she laughed

Showing stained teeth

Teeth that grinned,

And I grinned,

Like a vampire does,

What great frolics,

Liberated gluttony

On that sunny day

The Shape of it all

Shapes are too weird

I can never enjoy them

Neither cute nor warm

But too acute and cold

They live a strange life

Inadequate

Made up of lines and lengths

Or degrees of curve

They can't seem to concur

The triangle is an enigma

Does it strive for symmetry?

Or is it happy to be random?

It is too obtuse to see

Clifford Britten

Journey

Swept from my bed

In darkened skies.

You shook me

Grass underfoot

Like secret spies

You took me

safe journey

To a special place

You showed me

I was yours

For that brief space

You loved me

Seven Hours

Seven hours is a long time
To do stuff
Use it in the following ways
Carry out a vasectomy
Watch 3 west end plays
Endure 4 football games
Each one pretty much the same
See Ben Hur twice
Cocaine induced sex is nice
Write 12 poems
Listen to Bowie or Leonard Cohen
Bowie preferred
Just for the words
Seven hours later
On the 6th play it occurred
That those lyrics
Will taunt you
The Bewlay brothers haunt you, so.
Escape the moonage daydream
Get in the fashion mainstream
Go shopping buy clobber
Take it back again
Tomorrow
Seven hours is too long
To queue
For Sharon Osborne's autograph

Sixteen people

My sister she is sweet

My accountant's books are neat

My doctor always scares me

My lover often wears me

My bank manager's a bore

My landlord is a whore

My dentist's a real pain

My best friend is a strain

My lawyer is a crook

My neighbour is a cook

My auntie is so great

My uncle gets irate

My dad just loves a beer

My mum no longer here

My cousin she's so cool

My cousin he's a fool

My list is very short

My aim just to report

Clifford Britten

Out of this World

The Sun and the Moon go around together

They have been seeing each other a long time

They love each other

The Sun does day work

The Moon works at night

So they don't see each other that often

Which can help in a relationship

The Sun he is a bit of a show off, wide boy

But the Moon, she is cool and gentle

Sometimes when the Sun looks at the Moon in a certain way

She hides her face in shyness

When the clouds come out and cover them

The Moon and the Sun kiss

They have promised they will never leave each other

The Sun will always make the Moon shine

Fat Bloke

I knew this bloke

Who was a little bit fat?

And when he sat on his girlfriend's chair

He broke the leg in half

She went mad and said

Unless you wanna be dead

Go and get some "Evo stick"

And fix that leg

So he went to Stan's DIY

Apparently where they don't ever lie

And they told him he needs "Epoxy resin"

But the rules of the glue state

That when he uses it, 24 hours he must wait

So he goes back to his girlfriend

On the Monday with the glue

And tells her

I have to wait 24 hours

So will Tuesday do?

Cash crisis

My life is a series of months

If I live the average life span

I'll make it to 900,..   Months that is

Convert months to pounds

Not much, £900 is it?

Thing is I've already spent £648

Most unwisely

So I've got £252 left

My God!!!!!!   (Is that all?)

The other thing is

It's not in the bank making interest

I may only have 20 pence left if

I die sometime next week

Anyone know a good investment?

Drivel

I was listening to this radio talk in show

And this guy rang in

And what he was trying to say

In his articulate manner

Was, sort of like, erm

You know what I mean?

And obviously, you know

It's like

Well you know, it's like

Obviously, sort of

Anyway. Whatever

You know, sort of like

D'yer know what I mean?

It's like, It's like, it's erm

You know, obviously erm

It's like, sort of

Whatever, and erm

And do you know what?

The funny thing is

I knew what he was trying to say

Clifford Britten

The waiting game

The wasted space

Of futile, infertile, frantic moments

Gone, never to return

The essence of the wait….

The unknown length

The in limbo state

Of dull inaction

How much longer to wait ?

For the bus, train, cab

The barman to sort the tab

The very long-winded lunch

To queue behind a bunch

Of slovenly sloths

Who can't get off

The train too quick

In case they slip

Oh hurry up and make that tea

This waiting is annoying me

All I said was not too strong

I thought you had the kettle on

Lets go back then to the wait

The watch face, which will agitate

 Drumming fingers all rhythmic

How much longer, just a tick!

Come on! Come on!

No more of this

The voices in your head persist

Form a queue

It won't be long

I need a hand

Please move along

I'll just go get……..

Hold on a while

Its just that we…….

That sickly smile

Please take a seat

Be just a mo'

Just sign this

Before you go

And then they say

If you could, just please….

And have you falling to your knees

Clifford Britten

World Cup ················ A Repetitive Tale

32 teams enter fighting for the crown

After 48 matches there are 16 down

The 16 that remain enter the knockout stage

8 more depart here, most of them in a rage

one of them is England and they deserved to go

Leaving the supporters' morale at an all time low

Quarterfinals beckon, the real games begin

Red cards littered all around, it is such a sin

Now the semi finals, the elite final four

England's demise more apparent what a crushing bore

There's drama if you watch it

Leaves the final 2

Extra time and penalties

This tournament has flew

Crown the final victors

It's always the same

Tears and pointed fingers

The referee's to blame

Then wait a further four years

32 teams in brand new kit

The only thing that's guaranteed

England will be shit

New York

New York, New York
They named it twice
The casinos where I threw the dice
To win the cents,
And make some sense
Of the place Times Square
Where no one has any time to spare
I was all too eager to pay the fare
Of the bright yellow cabs
Driven by non yellow men
Who drink the tabs
In the bars along the grid like streets
Trodden by those many feet
With their dirty sheets
Hanging on the line
What I'm trying to say and define
Is straight streets, with mean cheats
Who buy fast food to eat and drink
And on fast food it makes you think
How it takes so long and how it stinks
And those shops called "Thrift"
That have the nerve
To charge so much for items served

Those prices they are ultra tight
And Central Park have you seen that sight?
It's not in the centre but to the right
And slightly north and not in the middle
Such confusion, Please why the riddle?
Broadway too is much the same
The street that belies its name
Although it's broad and very neat
It is no wider than any other street
And what's going on here with the sport
They haven't given that much thought
New York Yankees
Super team
Play in the World Series, what a dream
Trouble is it's just not fair
When no other countries' teams are there
So all in all I get confused
By this city, it leaves me bemused
So when they say
In their own special way
Thank you sir
Have a nice day
I can't

Short Story
One Way Mission

Once the exit door of the holding bay was closed there was darkness, but at least it was dry and warm and for the time being they were safe.

There were only twelve of them left now; it had been almost two hours ago that the last one had left., one minute he had been with the others, but then as the door to the holding bay opened the strange compelling force that had taken the rest of them had come for him. They each knew they were destined to play their part at some stage or other in this ritual and this increased their fears.

They had as yet been told nothing of the purpose of their mission, and because of this

The waiting had become unbearable.

The holding bay was still quite cramped even though several of them had departed.

Benson however had managed to sit away from the others as much as possible, enjoying the small amount of space he had created for himself.

He was concerned that none of the others who had left had managed to return and this worried him deeply

"Why had they not returned so as to let us know what was going on outside. Surely we would have to be told soon?" he thought.

" If not how will we know how to react when we are selected for departure?"

Benson pondered on this last thought as he sat waiting.

They all remained silent. Waiting, waiting for the holding bay door to open, and waiting to see who would be next.

They had been dispatched from their base the day before but none of them had been informed of their mission.

They all wore the same uniform of clinical white suits that covered them from head to foot, and each with special protective headgear.

Clifford Britten

To ease his mind Benson tried to think of the past but found it too difficult with the claustrophobic atmosphere of the holding bay bearing down on him. He could not manage to muster a single tangible thought of any importance.

All of his concentration centred on who would be next, they were all thinking this, all twelve of them that remained.

There was no pattern to gauge when the door would next open. Each time lapse had been different and this made the waiting all the more arduous.

They waited and waited none of them speaking, the strain on each of them intensifying with each passing moment. Who could tell how long it would be this time?

And then it happened the door to the holding bay opened quite quickly and without warning, the narrow exit allowing daylight into the chamber where they waited, and within a second one of them was pulled away by the strange force as before. The eleven that remained watched transfixed but relieved as the door to the holding bay began to close once more.

It was Benson who noticed it first. The door to the holding bay had not closed fully this time, a thin beam of light still shone through into their chamber. They could see through this small opening and what they saw chilled them.

Their comrade after leaving the holding bay had ascended for a while unhindered when suddenly a huge ball of white flame had engulfed him. The energy from the flame was so intense that the white protective suit he wore disintegrated almost immediately, and the heat from the flame so powerful that within a few moments all that remained of their comrade was a mass of glowing red embers. They watched in despair as the thick grey smoke rose upwards and left in its wake the most appalling stench.

They stared through the small opening in disbelief as the heat consumed him totally until all that remained was his protective headgear, which tumbled away smouldering into the distance.

The door to the holding bay then closed completely and they were in darkness again. It was as if the door had been deliberately left open in order that they may know their fate. "Had this happened to all the others"? Benson could not be sure but the fear rose inside him like a sickness.

The thoughts constant now, relentless, forever asking the questions.

The Kiss & The Bite

Who would be next, why were they here and what was the purpose of their mission, would they ever know?

Not much time had elapsed since the horror show, or maybe it just seemed that way as they tried to come to terms with what had happened, when the door of the holding bay opened again, more slowly this time and, daylight entered their chamber once more.

They looked up each of them with the same single thought. Please not me, not this time.

Benson could feel himself being pulled towards the opening. It was a strange sensation of weightlessness as he left the holding bay, he knew now that he had been chosen and that he would not survive, he also in an instant realised his mission and who he was. He thought back to the previous day. There were twenty of them then and they had stood side by side in their white suits together in the holding bay, proud of who they were but all of that was meaningless now as Benson awaited his fate, he looked back at the holding bay, the shining gold exterior and the government health warning that was written on its side were the last things he saw as the fiery white ball of heat came upwards and the flame engulfed him.

Smoking can damage your health.

Lightning Source UK Ltd.
Milton Keynes UK
UKOW051220070412

190286UK00001B/2/P